Lizzie and Harold

Story by Elizabeth Winthrop
Pictures by Martha Weston

Lothrop, Lee & Shepard Books
New York

Printed in the United States of America.

First Edition

1 2 3 4 5 6 7 8 9 10

Library of Congress Cataloging in Publication Data
Winthrop, Elizabeth.
    Lizzie and Harold.

    Summary: Lizzie wants a best friend more than any-
thing else, but, as she explains to Harold, who would
like to be her best friend, it must be a girl.
    [1. Friendship—Fiction]   I. Martha Weston, ill. II. Title.
PZ7.W768Liz 1986   [E]   83-14858
ISBN 0-688-02711-3
ISBN 0-688-02712-1 (lib. bdg.)

For Sasha and Peter
—E. W.

To my parents,
Nelson and Patty Hairston
—M. W.

More than anything else, Lizzie wanted a best friend.

"How do you get a best friend?" she asked her mother.

"You don't really *get* a best friend," her mother answered. "Usually they just happen if you wait."

But Lizzie did not want to wait.
She wanted a best friend right away.

"Today I am going to find my best friend,"
Lizzie told Harold.

Harold lived next door. Every day they walked
to school together.

"Why do you want a best friend?" Harold asked.

"Because I need someone to tell secrets to and
I want someone to teach me cat's cradle and I want

someone who likes me as much as I like her,"
Lizzie said.

"I'll be your best friend," Harold said.

"You can't be," Lizzie said. "You're a boy."

"So what?" said Harold.

But Lizzie did not answer.

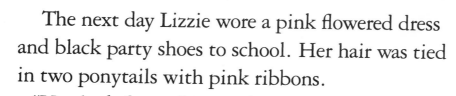

The next day Lizzie wore a pink flowered dress
and black party shoes to school. Her hair was tied
in two ponytails with pink ribbons.

"You look funny," Harold said.

"I look like Christina," Lizzie answered.
"She is going to be my new best friend."

"I like you best when you look like Lizzie,"
Harold said.

When Lizzie got to school, she ran up to Christina.

"Hello," said Lizzie. "I'm wearing my hair just like yours."

Christina did not answer.

"I'm wearing a dress and party shoes just like you," said Lizzie. "I brought a piece of string so you could teach me cat's cradle. I want you to be my best friend."

"I don't want a best friend," Christina said.

"You don't?" said Lizzie.
"No," said Christina.
She walked away.

"How's your new friend?" Harold asked on the way home.

"Don't ask," said Lizzie. "Christina's not my best friend after all."

"That was quick," said Harold.

"I have a new idea," Lizzie said.

"What is it?" Harold asked.

"You'll see," said Lizzie.

16

The next day, Lizzie put a sign on the front door of her house.

The doorbell rang. Lizzie ran to open it.

Wanted—One Best Friend. Must be a girl, six years old. Please ring door bell.

There stood Harold.

"Here I am," he said.
"Your new best friend."

"You can't be my best friend," Lizzie said.
"You're a boy, and you're only five and three quarters."

"I learned how to do cat's cradle," Harold said.

"You did?" Lizzie said. "Can you teach it to me?"

"Sure," Harold said.

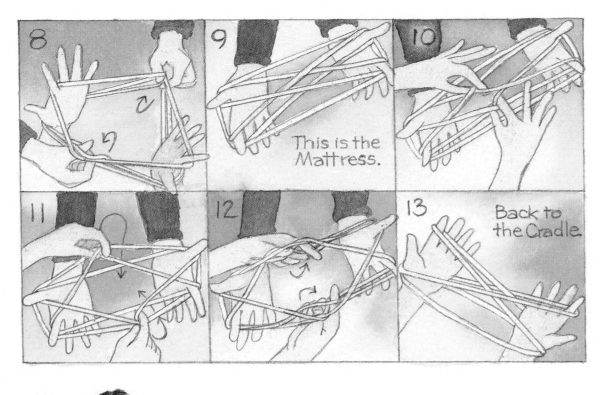

"I'll teach you Jacob's Ladder and Teacup and Saucer
and Witch's Hat tomorrow," Harold said.

Nobody else rang the doorbell.

Lizzie took down the sign.

"Does that mean I'm your best friend now?" Harold asked.

"No," said Lizzie. "That means I give up.
I don't want a best friend after all."

The next day Harold was carrying a big blue bag to school.

"What's in your bag?" asked Lizzie.

"It's my trick-or-treat candy," said Harold.

"Why are you taking it to school?" asked Lizzie.

"I'm going to give it to the person who promises to be my best friend," said Harold. "Since you don't want to be my best friend, I'm going to find somebody else."

"Harold, you can't find a best friend that way," Lizzie said.

"Why not?" asked Harold.

"Because best friends just happen to you. You can't go out and buy them. Besides, I thought you wanted to be *my* best friend," Lizzie cried.

But Harold wasn't listening.

All day long Lizzie thought about Harold. When she
met him after school, he did not have his blue bag
of candy.

"I have a new best friend," Harold said. "He is a boy.
He is five and a half years old. He ate all my candy and
his name is Douglas."

"Why do you look so sad?" Lizzie asked.
"Because I like you better," said Harold.

"Well, I have a new best friend too," Lizzie said.
"He is a boy. He is five and three quarters years old. He
knows how to do cat's cradle and he likes me as much
as I like him."

Harold looked even sadder.
"What's his name?" Harold asked.

"Harold," said Lizzie.